Songs and chants for ... phonics

SINGING PHONICS

Helen MacGregor
Catherine Birt

BOOK 2

whirr wihrr

toot toot

beep beep

ting-a-ling

Singalong CD

photocopiable

Supports the teaching of ...ters and Sounds

D1644374

C333935903

CONTENTS

SINGING PHONICS 2 © HELEN MACGREGOR & CATHERINE BIRT 2009 A&C BLACK PUBLISHERS LTD

SECTION 5 – CHEEKY CHIMP

SECTION 6 – SUNSET

SECTION 7 – HAPPY ENDINGS

MELODY LINES AND FLASHCARDS

First published 2009 by A&C Black Publishers Ltd,
Reprinted 2010, 2012, 2014
an imprint of Bloomsbury Publishing Plc
50 Bedford Square, London, WC1B 3DP
www.bloomsbury.com/music
Bloomsbury is a registered trademark of Bloomsbury Publishing Plc
Copyright © 2009 Helen MacGregor, Catherine Birt and A&C Black Publishers Ltd

ISBN: 978-1-4081-1451-3

Edited by Laura White
Designed by Fi Grant
Cover illustration © Sandra Isaksson 2009
Inside illustrations © Emily Skinner 2009
CD produced by Steve Grocott 2009
Performed by Kaz Simmons and Cleveland Watkiss

Printed in Great Britain by Ashford Colour Press Ltd

A&C Black uses paper produced with elemental chlorine-free pulp, harvested from managed sustainable forests.

INTRODUCTION

Singing Phonics 2 is the second in a series of songbooks bursting with stimulating, interactive and imaginative play-based activities designed to motivate and support the teaching of phonics in Foundation Stage and Key Stage 1.

The songs exemplify good practice in teaching phonics at Phases 2 and 3 of the Letters and Sounds programme, through multi-sensory approaches to stimulate deep learning. Each section in the songbook includes activities which support progression as set out in 'Letters and Sounds' (00281-2007 BKT-EN).

The songs and games provide further opportunities for the children to continue exploring sounds both aurally and orally, while following the systematic introduction of letters, word recognition and recall.

The Singing Phonics 2 songs

Many of the songs use traditional melodies written with new lyrics to enhance phonics work. There are also new chants and songs with original melodies in the book. The melody lines for all songs can be found on pages 62-71. The two chants (*The vowel song* and *Red Riding Hood rap*) do not have melody lines. Listen to the tracks on the CD.

The book is divided into seven sections which match the content of Phases 2 and 3:

SECTION 1 – YOO HOO HOO

SECTION 2 – ROCKET DOG

SECTION 3 – BIG BAD BUG

SECTION 4 – HAM AND JAM

SECTION 5 – CHEEKY CHIMP

SECTION 6 – SUNSET

SECTION 7 – HAPPY ENDINGS

About the activities
Using the songs and chants

The songs and activities in Singing Phonics 2 can and should be used in a variety of different ways:

Songs for listening

Use the CD to encourage children to join in with the vocal sounds or repeating patterns at the appropriate places, eg *Red Riding Hood rap*.

Songs for games

The practitioner should learn the songs and use them independently of the CD, adapting and extending them with props, letters, words or phonemes of their own choice to suit the needs of the class, eg *Pass the hat*.

Songs for children to sing

Encourage the children to learn by singing along with the CD and with you, so that they can sing the songs as a class or independently during child-initiated play, eg *Rocket dog*.

Child-initiated play

Use these ideas for indoor and outdoor play. The activities encourage the children to learn through play by exploring, consolidating and developing the letters, words and phonemes introduced in the songs.

Extend the activities

Here are some further ideas for developing the songs and games. These are suggestions which will challenge the children who are ready to progress on to more demanding activities. They aim to encourage you to discover more ideas of your own for extending the use of the songs and linking to, eg storybooks, drama and role-play, other curriculum areas and themes.

The teaching focus of each activity is summarised at the bottom of each page.

SINGING PHONICS 2 © HELEN MACGREGOR & CATHERINE BIRT 2009 A&C BLACK PUBLISHERS LTD

What you will need

The resources needed for each activity are listed in these boxes. Further resources are suggested in the 'Extend the activity' sections. You may wish to add your own ideas for useful resources to the 'What you will need' boxes.

The collection of flashcards on pages 72-80 (and throughout the book) can be photocopied and used for many of the activities. In Singing Phonics 2 you may copy any illustration as many times as necessary to create picture cards. Blank cards can be found on page 71. Use them to create your own cards.

The CD

Each of the songs can be found on the CD: the CD icon at the top of the page gives the track number.

A full track list can be found on the inside front cover of the book.

Phonics

01

Phase 2

Sections 1-3 in Singing Phonics 2 represent Phase 2 of 'Letters and Sounds.'

Phase 2 of 'Letters and Sounds' marks the beginning of systematic high quality phonic teaching and learning. Children entering Phase 2 should have experienced a variety of speaking and listening activities, and should be familiar with oral segmenting and blending of cvc (consonant/ vowel/ consonant) words such as c-a-t, cat; d-o-g, dog. They should have experienced fun with rhyme and rhythm and should be able to distinguish between general sounds all around them, not only the sounds that letters make.

Phase 2 of 'Letters and Sounds,' and Sections 1-3 of Singing Phonics 2 introduces children to 19 letters and moves from oral segmenting and blending to segmenting and blending with letters. Children quickly learn how to make simple words from the letters and sounds they are learning. There is a suggested order in which letters and sounds should be taught. The document states that 'automatic reading of words - decodable and tricky - is the ultimate goal'.

Phase 3

Sections 4-7 in Singing Phonics 2 represent Phase 3 of 'Letters and Sounds'.

Phase 3 of 'Letters and Sounds,' and Sections 4-7 of Singing Phonics 2 build on the 19 letters already learned and children's skills of segmenting to spell and blending to read.

One representation of the other 25 phonemes are taught in Phase 3, most of these comprising two letters making one phoneme (digraphs) such as ai in pain and oa in boat. They also learn the names of the letters and how to read and spell some tricky words. Once again, 'automatic reading of words - decodable and tricky - is the ultimate goal'.

Glossary of phonic terms

Phonics: is the knowledge and skills of segmenting and blending, knowledge of the alphabetic code and an understanding of how the code works in reading and spelling.

A phoneme: is the smallest unit of sound in a word. For example c-a-tch is made up of 3 phonemes making the word catch. There are 44 phonemes in the English language. Phonemes are represented by graphemes.

A grapheme: is the written symbol of a phoneme, that is a letter or more than one letter representing a sound or phoneme. For instance f-i-sh are the 3 graphemes representing the 3 phonemes in fish.

A digraph: is a two-letter grapheme making one sound or phoneme, for instance ea in beans or oo in spoon.

A trigraph: is a three-letter grapheme making one sound or phoneme, for instance igh in light.

Segmenting and blending: segmenting is breaking down words into their constituent phonemes to aid spelling. Blending is building words from their constituent phonemes to aid reading. Segmenting and blending should be seen as reversible processes and both skills are equally important for children to practise and learn.

CAN YOU SIT UPON A PIN?

01

Using the song

★ Familiarise the children with the song by singing it yourself, or using track 01.

★ Show the children each picture card in turn as the object is mentioned at the end of each line of the song.

★ Hold up the matching pairs of picture cards mentioned during the sound talk sections, eg pin and dog, tin and log, tin and pin, log and dog.

★ Place the four picture cards in order where the children can see them.

★ Teach the children both verses by singing a line and asking them to copy sing until they can sing the whole verse themselves.

★ During the sound talk sections invite the children or confident individuals to sound out the words.

What you will need

• A set of four picture cards showing each of the items mentioned in the song: pin, tin, dog, log (pg 7)

Child-initiated play

★ Leave the picture cards and/or artefacts where the children can play with them and sing the song for themselves.

★ Encourage the children to place the cards in new sequences and sing new verses, eg 'Can you sit upon a log?' and 'Do you like to pat the dog?'

Extend the activities

★ Use the picture cards and/or artefacts to practise oral segmentation and blending of each word with the children, eg t-i-n, tin.

★ Show the children individual letter cards (pgs 72-76) to help them form the words by segmenting and blending.

★ Place the letter cards for each word where the children can see them, then sing the song to reinforce the learning and introducing the grapheme-phoneme correspondences.

TEACHING FOCUS

★ Teaching grapheme/phoneme correspondences for p i n d o g t l
★ Manipulating above graphemes/phonemes into CVC words
★ Matching words to appropriate pictures

CAN YOU SIT UPON A PIN?

Can you sit upon a pin?
Do you like beans in a tin?
Do you like to pat the dog?
Can you sit upon a log?
Can you sound talk pin and dog?
P-i-n, pin, d-o-g, dog.
Can you sound talk tin and log?
T-i-n, tin, l-o-g, log.

Can you sit upon a tin?
Do you like beans on a pin?
Do you like to pat the log?
Can you sit upon a dog?
Can you sound talk tin and pin?
T-i-n, tin, p-i-n, pin.
Can you sound talk log and dog?
L-o-g, log, d-o-g, dog.

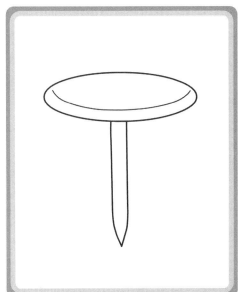

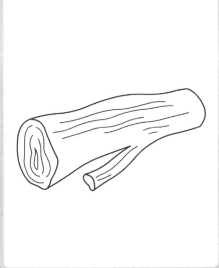

BEANS

TAP TAP TAP

02

Using the song

★ Listen to the song (track 02).

★ Teach the song one verse at a time, encouraging the children to perform the actions in the lyrics as you sing (eg tap knees for 'tap tap tap, upon your knee').

★ Discuss the words of the second verse and ask the children how they can sing this to reflect the meaning, ie using their voices quietly for 'Pad pad pad, make no sound.'

Child-initiated play

★ Once the children know the song, encourage them to perform their own actions indoors and outdoors.

★ Place teddies where the children can use the toys to enact the song as they sing it for themselves.

Extend the activities

★ Practise segmenting and blending the CVC words used in the song.

★ Use the vocabulary from the song, eg tap, pat, spin and pad, to promote knowledge and understanding in different contexts. For example, children might explore spinning tops, balls or be encouraged to dance with ribbons during physical play.

What you will need

• Four word cards – tap, pat, spin, pad (below and pg 9)

tap

TEACHING FOCUS

★ Grapheme/phoneme correspondences for s a t p i n d
★ Segmenting to spell and blending to read simple graphemes/phonemes

TAP TAP TAP

Tap tap tap, upon your knee.
Pat pat pat, count to three.
One two three, tap some more, then
Pat pat pat on the floor.

Spin spin spin, round and round.
Pad pad pad, make no sound.
One two three, spin some more, then
Pat pat pat on the floor.

Tap tap tap, upon your knee.
Pat pat pat, count to three.
One two three, tap some more,
then
Pat pat pat on the floor.

pat   spin   pad

PASS THE HAT

Using the song

★ Listen to the song (track 03).

★ Sit the children in a circle and ask them to listen carefully to the instructions in the song.

★ Place the letter cards in the hat. As the children listen they pass the hat round the circle, stopping in line three.

★ The child holding the hat selects a card and shows it to everyone. They say the sound on the card.

★ Repeat the game until several children have had a turn at choosing a card. Once the children are familiar enough with the song, encourage them to sing it by themselves.

Child-initiated play

★ Leave the hat and letter cards where the children can organise and play the game for themselves in small groups, indoors or outdoors. As they gradually become familiar with more sounds, add these to the collection of cards, eg i n m d, or g o c k.

★ Provide stimulating writing materials, indoors or outdoors as appropriate, eg crayons, chalk, squeezy bottles containing water or coloured water so that they can practise forming the letters for themselves.

Extend the activities

★ Play the game, this time inviting the individual who has selected the card to say the sound before all the children repeat the answer.

★ Extend the game by asking the children to suggest words that use the sound that has been chosen:

at the beginning of the word, eg s - sit, sat, set, supermarket,

in the middle of the word, eg a - hat, bag, pad, Saturday,

or at the end of the word eg t - mat, cut.

TEACHING FOCUS

★ Consolidating grapheme/phoneme correspondences for s a t p i n
★ Encouraging children to begin to write graphemes using a variety of implements

PASS THE HAT
Tune: Row, row, row your boat

Pass pass pass the hat,
Pass it round and round.
When it stops, take a card,
Can you say the sound?

YOO HOO HOO

Using the song

★ Listen to the song on track 04 and hold up each letter card as it is sounded out in the song (eg b, a and t for verse 1).

★ Teach the chorus first ('Oh, we can make a new word'), making sure the children understand how to blend the sounds in the last line. Then sing the verse (using track 04 if you need to) and ask the children to join in with the repeated lines of the chorus and the blending.

★ Teach the verses one by one. Ask three children to stand in line and hold up the individual letter cards at the appropriate times and then form the word in the last line.

Child-initiated play

★ Place pictures or objects of a bat, a pen and the sun together with the letter cards (suggested in the 'what you will need' box), or put magnetic letters in an attractive bag or box for children to experiment with during play.

★ At a later stage further artefacts/letters/magnetic letters from the extension activities could be added or substituted, for children to play with.

Extend the activities

★ Place the recording of the song and the letter cards where the children can listen and make the words for themselves as they join in.

★ Make up new verses with the children using CVC words they are learning about in their phonics work. As they gradually learn more complex phonemes, add these too, eg d - o -ll, b - oo - t, g - oa - t, sh - o - p. Use phonemes on cards so that the children can explore making up new verses for themselves (pgs 71-80).

★ You may like to add picture cards to see if the children can use the phonemes you provide to select, sound out, and form whole words.

What you will need

• A set of letter cards/magnetic letters to make each word, eg b a t p e n s u (pgs 72-76)

• A bag or a box containing pictures or objects of a bat, a pen and the sun

• Photocopy any illustration in the book to create picture cards and use blank cards (pg 71)

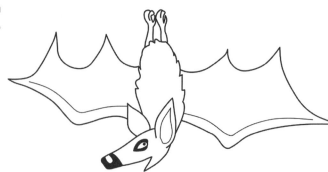

TEACHING FOCUS

★ Segmenting to spell and blending to read words made up of graphemes/ phonemes s a t p n and b e u

★ Listening to where certain phonemes are in CVC words—beginning, middle or end

YOO HOO HOO

Tune: The Hokey Cokey

You say the b sound first,
And then the a sound too.
You finish with the t sound and give a yoo hoo hoo!
You put the sounds together then you wait and see,
What will the new word be?

Chorus:
Oh, we can make a new word,
Oh, we can make a new word,
Oh, we can make a new word,
b – a – t makes bat, you see!

You say the p sound first,
And then the e sound too,
You finish with the n sound and give a yoo hoo hoo!
You put the sounds together then you wait and see,
What will the new word be?

Chorus:
Oh, we can make a new word,
Oh, we can make a new word,
Oh, we can make a new word,
p – e – n makes pen, you see!

You say the s sound first,
And then the u sound too.
You finish with the n sound and give a yoo hoo hoo!
You put the sounds together then you wait and see,
What will the new word be?

Chorus:
Oh, we can make a new word,
Oh, we can make a new word,
Oh, we can make a new word,
s – u – n makes sun, you see!

TICK TOCK

05

Using the song

★ Listen to the song on track 05 together and talk about the times of day mentioned in each verse.

★ Play the song again and ask the childre to join in with the 'tick tock' in each verse. Teach the song one verse at a time, using track 05 or by singing the song yourself.

★ When the children are familiar with all verses, sing the song all the way through. Show the time on a clock face during each verse.

Child-initiated play

★ Once the children are familiar with the song, leave as many types of toy and real clocks around for them to play with.

★ Pictures suggested above could be laminated for children to practise sequencing the daily activities in the song, along with times on the clocks.

Extend the activities

★ Teach the children other o'clock times, discussing possible activities in their daily routine that would match these and making up other verses for the song appropriate to them.

★ This would reinforce the phoneme/grapheme ck in clock, o'clock, tick, tock and would encourage children to apply phonic skills and knowledge across other areas of learning (Knowledge and Understanding, Problem Solving, Reasoning and Numeracy, Personal Social and Emotional Development).

What you will need

• A toy clock with moveable fingers

• Simple pictures containing various clocks, and depicting a child in the bedroom getting dressed, in the kitchen eating lunch, in the playroom having tea, and in the bedroom in bed

tick

tock

TEACHING FOCUS

★ Teaching grapheme/phoneme correspondence for *ck*
★ Making and reading words using *ck*
★ Sequencing children's patterns of activity during the day using vocabulary such as clocks and 'tick tock'

TICK TOCK

In my bedroom hangs a clock,
It wakes me up at eight o'clock.
Tick tock tick tock sings my clock,
Time to rise at eight o'clock.

In my kitchen hangs a clock,
It chimes for lunch at twelve o'clock.
Tick tock tick tock chimes my clock,
Time for lunch at twelve o'clock.

In my playroom hangs a clock,
It calls cuckoo at four o'clock.
Tick tock tick tock cuckoo clock,
Time for tea at four o'clock.

In my bedroom hangs a clock,
Bedtime comes at seven o'clock.
Tick tock tick tock sings my clock,
Time for bed at seven o'clock.

RUN RAT RUN

06

Using the song

★ Sing the song to the children, or play track 06 as you act out the words with the toy animals.

★ Encourage the children to join in, using their hands and fingers to mime the actions of the imaginary animals on their bodies. Ask them to join in singing the last two lines of each verse:

> Up down, up down,
> Run rat run.

★ Teach them the whole song gradually, as they become familiar with the way it 'grows' in each verse.

Child-initiated play

★ Leave the toys or picture cards where the children can play independently and sing the song for themselves.

★ Encourage the children to use the toys outdoors to physically enact the song in a large space, moving up and down using their whole bodies and running at the end of each verse.

Extend the activities

★ Use the CVC words from the song by orally segmenting and blending. Make a set of letter cards for the words: pet, rat, cat, bit, run, dog, leg, ran. Use the blank cards on pg 77 if you want to create your own flashcards.

★ Work with the children to form the letter cards into the CVC words from the song.

★ Sing the song again, using the completed words to reinforce grapheme-phoneme correspondence.

★ Make up new verses to increase aural memory as the list grows, eg 'My pet pig pushed my pet dog...'

What you will need

• Toys or finger puppets: rat, cat, dog - or picture cards of each animal (pg 17)

TEACHING FOCUS

★ Manipulating familiar graphemes/ phonemes from section 1 - s a t p i n, with some new graphemes/ phonemes from section 2 - g o c e u r, to make new CVC words

★ Having fun with rhyming words in an action song

RUN RAT RUN

My pet rat ran up my leg,
My pet rat ran down again.
Up down, up down,
Run rat run.

My pet cat bit my pet rat,
My pet rat ran up my leg,
My pet rat ran down again.
Up down, up down,
Run rat run.

My pet dog chased my pet cat,
My pet cat bit my pet rat,
My pet rat ran up my leg,
My pet rat ran down again.
Up down, up down,
Run rat run.

ROCKET DOG

07

Using the song

★ Listen to the song on track 07 or sing it to the children, performing actions to illustrate the story as you sing. Encourage them to join in straight away with the actions and the repeating lines (when both voices are heard).

★ Share and copy the descriptive actions that individual children devise as you sing the song again.

★ Sing the song several times until the children are familiar with the words and enjoy making their own actions.

Child-initiated play

★ Leave a variety of materials around for children to build either a large rocket and/or individual rockets (for instance: shiny silver paper, large and small boxes, cardboard tubes, coloured paper and card, felt tip pens, paints, buttons and milk bottle tops, items to make levers for controls).

★ Alternatively, a role-play area could be made into a space rocket, with the help of the children. The story of the song could be acted out by the children, reinforcing the phoneme ck in words rocket, pocket, ticket, packed, as well as reinforcing CVC words such as mum, dad, bed, hug, kiss.

Extend the activities

★ Use the first lines of the song to help the children substitute known and new words for the word dog, eg 'My rat went up in a rocket' or 'My pig took me in her pocket' This would also encourage children to use alliterative phrases.

What you will need

• Materials to build a large rocket or individual rockets (see 'Child-initiated play')

TEACHING FOCUS

★ Familiarising children with all graphemes/ phonemes in section 1 and section 2
  - s a t p i n g o c k ck e u r, with a particular emphasis on ck, r and g
★ Using new graphemes in simple CVC words, as well as in more advanced words such as rocket, pocket, ticket, packed

ROCKET DOG

Tune: The bear went over the mountain

My dog went up in a rocket,
My dog went up in a rocket,
He bought a ticket and packed a bag,
And then he waved goodbye.
And then he waved goodbye,
And then he waved goodbye,
He bought a ticket and packed a bag,
And then he waved goodbye.

My cat went up on a carrot, (x2)
She bought a ticket and packed a bag,
And then she waved goodbye.
And then she waved goodbye, (x2)
She bought a ticket and packed a bag,
And then she waved goodbye.

My dad went up in an egg cup, (x2)
He bought a ticket and packed a bag,
And then he waved goodbye.
And then he waved goodbye, (x2)
He bought a ticket and packed a bag,
And then he waved goodbye.

My mum took me in her pocket, (x2)
We bought a ticket and packed a bag,
And then we waved goodbye.
And then we waved goodbye, (x2)
We bought a ticket and packed a bag,
And then we waved goodbye.

We all came back on a Sunday, (x2)
We said hello with a hug and kiss,
And then we went to bed.
And then we went to bed, (x2)
We said hello with a hug and kiss,
And then we went to bed.

SAD MAD CATS

Using the song

★ Listen to the song on track 08 and all join in with marching actions to the steady beat.

★ Listen again and join in with the patterns in the fourth line of the song, eg Meow meow, meow meow.

★ Finally, teach all of the verses one at a time. When the children are familiar with the song, divide them into four groups - cats, ants, dogs and rats - and invite each group to sing and act out their own verse to create a class performance.

Child-initiated play

★ Provide suitable materials for children to make half-face animal masks for the cats, ants, dogs and rats so that they can act out the story in role play.

★ Encourage the children to use drums and beaters to tap out marching rhythms.

Extend the activities

★ Using individual white boards and pens, ask the children to sound talk each word in turn - cat, hat, ant, dog, clog, rat – to spell and write.

★ Blend the phonemes together to read the words.

★ Ask the children to change the words into plural by adding 's'.

What you will need

- Individual white boards and pens
- Resources for animal masks
- Drums and beaters

TEACHING FOCUS

★ Using and applying most graphemes/ phonemes s a t p i n, and g o c k ck e u r
★ Manipulating phonemes/graphemes into simple CVC words - cat, hat, ant, dog, clog, rat
★ Raising awareness of plurals by adding s to CVC and CCVC words

SAD MAD CATS

Sad mad cats,
In black silk hats,
Are marching in to town.
Meow meow, meow meow,
Marching up and down.

Small black ants,
In underpants,
Are marching in to town.
Left right, left right,
Marching up and down.

Big bad dogs,
In bright pink clogs,
Are marching in to town.
Wuff wuff, wuff wuff,
Marching up and down.

Rare rich rats,
In smart top hats,
Are marching in to town.
Squeak squeak, squeak squeak,
Marching up and down.

SINGING PHONICS 2 © HELEN MACGREGOR & CATHERINE BIRT 2009 A&C BLACK PUBLISHERS LTD

THE VOWEL SONG

Using the song

★ Learn the song yourself using track 09.

★ Introduce the children to the first verse only when they are learning about short vowel sounds. Encourage them to call out the short vowel sounds in response to the instructions as indicated on the songsheet (pg 23).

★ Choose five children to stand in a line, holding one vowel each in the same order as they appear in the song. As the children sing each line, the vowel cards are held up for everyone to see.

★ When appropriate, use verse two to explore long vowel sounds in words.

What you will need

• Magnetic letters or letter cards representing the five vowels a e i o u (pgs 72-75)

Child-initiated play

★ Leave magnetic letters and/or letter cards representing the five vowels for the children to play with.

★ It would also be useful to have artefacts or pictures with matching words of items containing one of the short vowel sounds so that children could explore the short vowel sounds at the beginning and middle of words - ant, egg, pin, frog, bun.

Extend the activities

★ The second verse of this song would be better used at a later stage, when children are learning long vowel phonemes such as ee, oo, ai for instance.

★ As an extension activity at this stage, the children could listen to verse two to identify and say the long vowel sounds in words such as moon, rain and feet.

TEACHING FOCUS

★ Articulating phonemes for five short vowel sounds and recognising the graphemes
★ Exploring the position of short vowel sounds - beginning or middle, eg ant, cat

THE VOWEL SONG

Give me an a — a
Give me an e — e
Give me an i o u — i o u

Where are the short vowels?
We've got the short vowels

a e i o u.

Give me an a — a
Give me an e — e
Give me an i o u – i o u

Where are the long vowels?
We've got the long vowels

a e i o u.

BIG BAD BUG

Using the song

★ Play track 10 or sing the song to the children, encouraging them to join in every time they hear the buzz buzz pattern.

★ Sing the song again, showing the artefacts or picture cards to illustrate the story at the appropriate times to familiarise the children with the words. Teach the whole song a verse at a time.

★ Can the children find all the words in the song which begin with b? (big, bad, bug, beg, bed, bottom, buzz).

★ Can they identify the rhyming words? (bug, rug.)

Child-initiated play

★ Place appropriate toys or picture cards where children can play freely with them while singing the song and acting out the story.

★ Leave materials where the children can make their own bug, bed and rug, eg fabric, small boxes, tissue paper, pipe cleaners, buttons.

Extend the activities

★ Explore the vocabulary in the song – big, bad, bug, bed, rug - by orally segmenting and blending, eg b-i-g, big, then using letter cards to make the words.

★ Use the completed word cards and invite the children to match them to the toys or picture cards.

★ Explore other vocabulary by making up new verses of your own to sing with the children, eg 'There's a slinky, silver snake and its sitting on my seat, ssss ssss'.

What you will need

• Three artefacts or cards for the words: bug, bed and rug (below, pg 25 and pgs 72-80)

• Word card – buzz (pg 25)

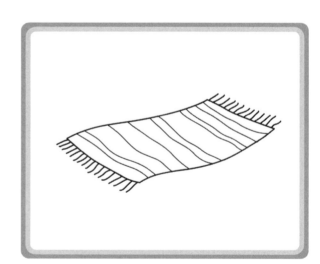

TEACHING FOCUS

★ Reinforcing an understanding of alliteration, words beginning with the same phoneme/grapheme

★ Exploring new phoneme/grapheme b and introducing zz

BIG BAD BUG

There's a big bad bug at the bottom of my bed,
Buzz buzz,   buzz buzz.

There's a big bad bug at the bottom of my bed,
Buzz buzz,   buzz buzz.

Bug on a bed, bug on a bed,
Buzz buzz,   buzz buzz.

I beg you bug, get off my bed,
Buzz buzz,   buzz buzz.

Go sit on the rug, that's the
place for a bug,
Buzz buzz,   buzz buzz.

Bug on a rug, bug on a rug,
Buzz buzz,   buzz buzz.

buzz
buzz

buzz

DOUBLES

Using the song

★ Show the children the letter cards l and ll. Encourage the children to identify the difference, ie two letters making the same phoneme as a single letter.

★ Now sound out the phonemes for each word: h-u-ff, p-u-ff, st-u-ff. Ask the children to orally blend the sounds to make the three words.

★ Show the children the word cards – huff, puff, stuff (pg 27) and all practise reading each word.

★ Teach the children the first verse by singing it yourself or play track 11.

★ Repeat the same process with the other verses over a number of sessions, until the children are familiar with the whole song.

Child-initiated play

★ Place pictures of the sound sources you collected where the children can use them to make new sequences and explore performing the sounds with their voices.

★ Prompt them to explore sounds with other themes using toys, pictures or percussion instruments as a stimulus eg creatures/ minibeasts, animals, transport, musical instruments.

Extend the activities

★ Put the word cards for one verse or eventually the whole song into a bag or box.

★ Encourage the children to explore the cards and orally segment and blend and practise reading the cards for themselves.

★ Leave writing equipment, eg whiteboard and pens, paper and crayons, chalk, squeezy bottle containing water, for the children to practise writing, indoors or outdoors.

What you will need

• Letter cards – f, ff, l, ll, s, ss, z, zz (pgs 72-80)

• Word cards: huff puff stuff well shell bell kiss miss hiss buzz fizz fuzz (see pgs 25, 27 and 72-80)

• Remember you can use the blank cards on pg 71 to create your own flashcards

TEACHING FOCUS

★ Introducing new digraphs (two letters making one phoneme) - ff, ll, ss, and zz
★ Recognising that two letters can make one phoneme - ff, ll, ss, zz
★ Segmenting to spell and blending to read words containing the digraphs above

DOUBLES
Tune: Jelly on a plate

Doubles at the end
Doubles at the end,
Double ff, that says f,
In huff and puff and stuff.

Doubles at the end,
Doubles at the end,
Double ll, that says l,
In well and shell and bell.

Doubles at the end,
Doubles at the end,
Double ss, that says s,
In kiss and miss and hiss.

Doubles at the end,
Doubles at the end,
Double zz, that says z,
In buzz and fuzz and fizz.

huff

stuff

puff

SECRET ANIMAL

Using the song

★ Show the three animals and ask children to identify them. Then, hide the animals from sight.

★ Play track 12, joining in with the animal noises and reveal the matching animal toy at the end of line six.

★ Now teach the children the song, inviting a child to select the matching animal in each verse.

★ Play the game with the children, singing any verse of the song yourself. Can the children supply the animal sounds for the song and choose the matching toy?

Child-initiated play

★ Place the toys where the children can play the game for themselves. Add other animals so that they can make up new verses and animal sounds.

Extend the activities

★ Play the game showing the children word cards for each of the animal sounds as you sing hop, hiss, huff, puff.

★ Ask the children to orally segment and blend each word.

   eg   h – o – p, hop.

★ With the children, choose instruments to replace the animal sounds in the song,

   eg   woodblock - hop,

   maracas - hiss,

   drum - huff puff.

★ Use other animals and sound cards,

   eg   cow - moo,

   dog - woof,

   owl - hoot,

   frog - croak,

   bear - growl.

TEACHING FOCUS

★ Consolidating recognition and use of digraphs ss, ff
★ Using known graphemes to orally segment and blend words such as hiss, huff, hop and puff

SINGING PHONICS 2 © HELEN MACGREGOR & CATHERINE BIRT 2009 A&C BLACK PUBLISHERS LTD

SECRET ANIMAL
Tune: Wind the bobbin up

Secret animal, secret animal,
Hop hop   hop hop hop.
Secret animal, secret animal,
Hop hop   hop hop hop.

See all the animals one two three,
Wolf, snake, rabbit – which will it be?   (spoken) It's the rabbit!
See all the animals one two three,
Wolf, snake, rabbit – which will it be?   (spoken) It's the rabbit!
Secret animal, secret animal,
Hop hop   hop hop hop.

Secret animal, secret animal,
Hiss hiss   hiss hiss hiss. (repeat)
See all the animals one two three,
Wolf, snake, rabbit – which will it be?   (spoken) It's the snake!
(repeat)
Secret animal, secret animal,
Hiss hiss   hiss hiss hiss.

Secret animal, secret animal,
Huff puff   huff huff puff. (repeat)
See all the animals one two three,
Wolf, snake, rabbit – which will it be?   (spoken) It's the wolf!
(repeat)
Secret animal, secret animal,
Huff puff   huff huff puff.

hop   hiss

ALPHABET

Using the song

★ Show the children an enlarged copy of the alphabet rainbow (pg 31).

★ Sing the song to the children, or use track 13, pointing to the letters one at a time.

★ Ensure that children understand that these are the names of the letters and not the sounds that they make.

★ Teach the children the song, then sing it frequently on other occasions so that they are confident at singing it by themselves.

Child-initiated play

★ Enlarge and place the alphabet rainbow at a level where the children can touch the letters as they explore the letter names and alphabet sequence.

★ Make magnetic letters available so that children can match the graphemes as they sing the song.

Extend the activities

★ Sing other alphabet songs and share alphabet books with the children.

★ Use familiar tunes to sing the alphabet, putting the stress on different groupings of letters, eg 'Jack and Jill', 'Mary Mary quite contrary','This old man'. Try singing the alphabet to these tunes, starting from other letters in the sequence so that the children become very familiar with all the letters as well as being able to sing starting at a.

★ Use other alphabet posters and resources (eg picture books) with upper and lower case letters to familiarise the children with both written forms.

What you will need

• Photocopiable illustration of an alphabet rainbow (pg 31)

• Letter cards a-z (pgs 72-76)

TEACHING FOCUS

★ Familiarising children with the sequence of letters in the alphabet
★ Familiarity with names of letters of the alphabet, so that children have the correct vocabulary
   to refer to letters making digraphs (2 letters making 1 phoneme) and trigraphs (3 letters making 1 phoneme)

ALPHABET

a b c, d e f,
g h i, j.
k l m, n o p,
q r s, t.
u v w,
x y z.

Al-pha-bet.

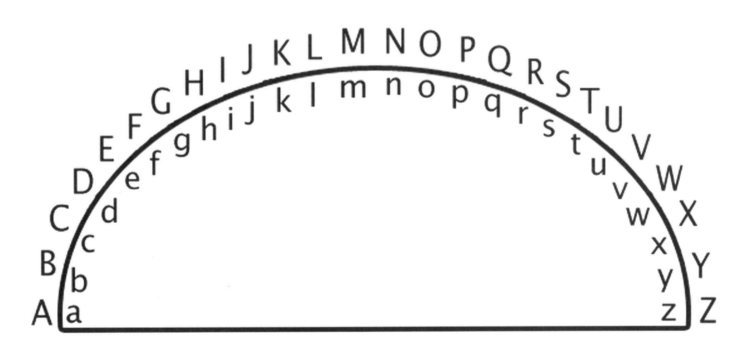

TWENTY SIX LETTERS

Using the song

★ Place the alphabet rainbow (pg 31) where the children can clearly see it. All listen to the song on track 14.

★ Talk about the difference between the letter names and the sounds that each letter makes.

★ Use the second verse to illustrate forming the word cat using separate magnetic letters or letter cards as you sing (pgs 72-76). Sing the song with the children, choosing your own CVC words and demonstrating with the letters.

Child-initiated play

★ Make available a selection of high quality alphabet books, magnetic letters, letters on cards, alphabet rainbow and a variety of mark making materials for children to play with in a book area or role-play area.

★ Give the children ample opportunities to explore letters and sounds in their own way through play.

★ Encourage them to sing the song and play the game, forming their own CVC words using the letters.

Extend the activities

★ With the help of the children, add new words to the last verse, asking the children to segment to spell and blend to read the new words, eg

     b-i-n, bin

     g-e-t, get

What you will need

• Alphabet rainbow (pg 31)

• Magnetic letters or letter cards on familiar phonemes to make into CVC words (pgs 72-80)

TEACHING FOCUS

★ Learning letter names
★ Consolidating understanding of phonemes and corresponding graphemes
★ Segmenting to spell and blending to read new words

TWENTY SIX LETTERS

Tune: Ten green bottles

Twenty six letters in the alphabet,
Twenty six letters in the alphabet,
Forty four phonemes,
This is what we get!

Twenty six letters in the alphabet.

Can you say the phonemes?
(spoken) c – a – t,
Can you say the phonemes?
(spoken) c – a – t,

Blend the sounds together,
And let's see what we get.

(Spoken) c – a – t,
(sing) to make the new word cat.

HAM AND JAM

Using the song

★ Play track 15 to the children or sing the song yourself.

★ Teach the first verse, one line at a time, showing the children the matching word cards and familiarising them with the two rhyming CVC names. Point out the use of capital letters for the two names.

★ Gradually teach the other two verses in the same way. Discuss how the last verse uses four CVC words in different orders, reinforcing this by showing the children the word cards.

Child-initiated play

★ Place all the word cards where the children can read and order them as they sing the song. Can they change the order of the words to match the changes in different lines? Prompt them to explore sounds with other themes using toys, pictures or percussion instruments as a stimulus, eg creatures/minibeasts, animals, transport, musical instruments.

Extend the activities

★ Play sound buttons with the children:

Invite individual children to draw a sound button under each phoneme for the CVC words used in the song, eg

s   a   m
● ● ●

What you will need

• Word cards - Pam Sam, sun fun, ham jam (below and pgs 35 & 80)

ham

TEACHING FOCUS

★ Identifying and reading rhyming words
★ Segmenting to spell and blending to read
★ Consolidating grapheme/phoneme correspondences

SINGING PHONICS 2 © HELEN MACGREGOR & CATHERINE BIRT 2009 A&C BLACK PUBLISHERS LTD

HAM AND JAM

I like Pam and I like Sam,
Pam and Sam like me.
Pam and Sam or Sam and Pam,
They're my pals you see!
Pam Sam Sam Pam,
Pam and Sam like me.
Pam Sam Sam Pam,
They're my pals you see!

You like sun and you like fun,
Sun and fun for you.
Sun and fun or fun and sun,
That's what I like too!
Sun fun fun sun,
Sun and fun for you.
Sun fun fun sun,
That's what I like too!

Pam likes ham and Sam likes jam,
Ham and jam for tea.
Ham and jam with Pam and Sam,
That's the tea for me!
Ham jam Pam Sam,
Ham and jam for tea.
Jam ham Sam Pam,
That's the tea for me!

jam

Pam

DIZZY THE DINOSAUR

16

Using the song

★ Play track 16 to the children.

★ Teach the first verse, one line at a time, reinforcing the use of a capital letter for the name, Dizzy.

★ Gradually teach the other two verses, with the names Dolly and Danny, as well as dicussing alliteration.

★ Once the children know the song, encourage them to act out the three verses while singing the song, giving each dinosaur different characteristics (as suggested in verses).

Child-initiated play

★ Set up a role-play area with a dinosaur theme. Encourage the children to sing the song themselves performing the actions, indoors and outdoors, and using the toys and puppets to enact the song.

Extend the activities

★ Use a sand or water tray to re-enact the song using the toys.

Re-create your own scene in a box using a variety of materials, eg play dough, paper, card.

★ Explore the descriptive vocabulary of the dinosaurs' movements with the children, pointing out the alliterative phrases, eg 'wobbly waddling'.

★ Encourage children to think of other names and characteristics for dinosaurs, beginning with different graphemes, for instance 'Sammy the Stegosaurus stomping all day' or 'Tilly the Triceratops tripping all day'.

What you will need

• Small toy/model dinosaurs, puppets

• Fiction and non-fiction picture books

TEACHING FOCUS

★ Using new phonemes/graphemes w j v zz y
★ Using adjacent consonants in more complex words, eg st - in stopping and stomping
★ Reinforcing alliteration (words beginning with the same phoneme/grapheme)

DIZZY THE DINOSAUR

Dizzy the dinosaur dancing all day,
Dizzy the dinosaur dancing this way,
Jerky jiving,
Wobbly waddling,
Busy bopping,
Not even stopping.
Dizzy the dinosaur dancing all day,
Dizzy the dinosaur dancing this way.

Dolly the dinosaur eating all day,
Dolly the dinosaur eating this way,
Noisy nibbling,
Careful crunching,
Perfect popping,
Not even stopping.
Dolly the dinosaur eating all day,
Dolly the dinosaur eating this way.

Danny the dinosaur playing all day,
Danny the dinosaur playing this way,
Clever climbing,
Steady stomping,
Happy hopping,
Not even stopping.
Danny the dinosaur playing all day,
Danny the dinosaur playing this way.

CHEEKY CHIMP

Using the song

★ Show the children each of the toys as you play track 17 or sing the song yourself.

★ Teach the first verse, showing them the appropriate ch digraph (two letters making one phoneme).

★ Can the children find all of he words beginning with ch? (cheeky, chimp, chases, children). Teach the other verses in the same way until the children can sing the whole song.

★ Use the instrumental verse to make up words, eg

'Here's a happy hen who has a handbag.'

Child-initiated play

★ Place the toys where the children can play with them and act out the words as they sing the song for themselves.

★ Encourage the children to act out the verses themselves indoors or outdoors, eg moving like a chimpanzee, a chick, and a sheep.

★ Leave the letter cards and toys where the children can match them together and use them to remind them of the verses of the song, singing it for themselves.

Extend the activities

★ Find other vocabulary using the ch, sh, th digraphs at the beginning, middle or end, eg chip, church, fisherman.

★ Play word-sort games to group words containing the same digraphs.

What you will need

• A toy or finger puppet of the four animals mentioned in the song (or picture cards): chimp, chick, sheep, and an unusual creature for the 'thingamajig'

• A set of letter cards – ch sh th (pgs 39 & 77)

TEACHING FOCUS

★ Consolidating known phonemes/graphemes ck, and short vowels
★ Introducing new digraphs (two sounds making one phoneme) – ch, sh, th
★ Matching digraphs - ch sh and th - to appropriate toys, pictures and words
★ Alliteration

CHEEKY CHIMP

Here's a cheeky chimp who chases children,
Chases children, chases children.
Here's a cheeky chimp who chases children,
Ch, ch, cheeky chimp.

Here's a charming chick whose chirps are cheerful,
Chirps are cheerful, chirps are cheerful.
Here's a charming chick whose chirps are cheerful,
Ch, ch, cheerful chick.

Here's a shaggy sheep who needs a shave,
Needs a shave, needs a shave.
Here's a shaggy sheep who needs a shave,
Sh, sh, shaggy sheep.

Instrumental verse

Here's a thingamajig who thinks of things,
Thinks of things, thinks of things.
Here's a thingamijig who thinks of things,
Th, th, thinks of things.

SH!

Using the song

★ Play the game 'What's in the box?': Show the children the card of the sh digraph (two letters making one phoneme) on pg 77.

Listen to track 18. Hold up each object when it is mentioned in the song (eg fish in verse one, ship in verse two, shell in verse three and shark in verse four).

Choose an object from the box without showing it to the children. Give them a clue using the words of the song so that they can identify which object you have chosen, eg 'it has fins and a tail and swims in the sea' (fish).

Children segment and blend the sounds in the song.

What you will need

• Fish, ship, shell and shark in a box (you can use objects or pictures)

• Letter cards – ch, sh (pgs 39 & 77)

Child-initiated play

★ Leave the box of objects named in the song for the children to play with as they explore singing the verses.

★ Set up a role-play area with a sea theme using other artefacts, eg fishing boat, fishing net, shells, shrimp, starfish, as well as objects using other phonemes.

Extend the activities

★ Find other objects using the sh or ch digraph cards.

★ Find other words/objects to play 'What's in the box?'

Children give clues to each other, for instance, 'it has wings and a beak and is yellow, what's in the box?' (a chick).

TEACHING FOCUS

★ Reinforcing the sh phoneme
★ Hearing and saying sounds in words in the order in which they occur
★ Matching phonemes/graphemes to pictures, artefacts, word cards

SH!

My mystery box has something to hide,
The phoneme is sh somewhere inside,
With fins and a tail, it swims in the sea,
What do you think this sh word can be?
(Spoken) It's a f-i-sh - fish.

My mystery box has something to hide,
The phoneme is sh somewhere inside,
It cuts through the waves and sails on the sea,
What do you think this sh word can be?
(Spoken) It's a sh-i-p - ship.

My mystery box has something to hide,
The phoneme is sh somewhere inside,
It's found on the shore, washed up by the sea,
What do you think this sh word can be?
(Spoken) It's a sh-e-ll - shell.

My mystery box has something to hide,
The phoneme is sh somewhere inside,
With very sharp teeth and a fin that scares me,
What do you think this sh word can be?
(Spoken) It's a sh-ar-k - shark!

KING PING PONG

What you will need

- Card with the digraph ng (below)
- Illustration of King Ping Pong and penguins (see pg 43)

Using the song

★ Ask the children to listen to the song on track 19.

★ Join in with the echos (sung by the male voice alone).

★ Teach them the chorus (sung by both voices together).

★ Show them an enlarged illustration from page 43. What do the children notice about King Ping Pong? (He is a penguin.) Can they find the ng sound in the word penguin?

★ Teach them the chorus and encourage them to join in each time it is repeated. Teach the verses one at a time.

Child-initiated play

★ Leave a crown, cloak and set of hand bells for children to act out the penguin story as they listen to track 19 or sing the song.

★ They can explore penguin movements as they play.

Extend the activities

★ Play the phoneme frame (see below) to emphasise understanding that two letters can make one phoneme (a digraph):

★ Draw a large 3-phoneme frame on a whiteboard. Say one of the ng words to the children in sound talk, eg p– i–ng, p–o–ng.

★ Ask a child to write the word, placing each phoneme in the correct part of the frame. Blend the sounds together to read the word.

p	i	ng
k	i	ng

★ Once the children are familiar with the process, they can play this on individual white boards.

KING PING PONG

Long ago there was a king,
A king who liked to sing,
A king who liked to sing.
Long ago there was a king,
He was a singing king,
He was a singing king.
Ping Pong, King Ping Pong,
Let all the bells ring for Ping Pong our king,
King Ping Pong.

Every day the people said,
'O King, please sing a song' (x2)
Every day the people said,
'And may we sing along?' (x2)
Ping Pong, King Ping Pong,
Let all the bells ring for Ping Pong our king,
King Ping Pong.

Ping Pong was a wise old king,
He let them sing along (x2)
Ping Pong was a wise old king,
They all joined in the song (x2)
Ping Pong, King Ping Pong,
Let all the bells ring for Ping Pong our king,
King Ping Pong.

So everyone was happy then,
Because they liked to sing (x2)
So everyone was happy then,
For singing was their thing! (x2)
Ping Pong, King Ping Pong,
Let all the bells ring for Ping Pong our king,
King Ping Pong.

THIS WAY, THAT WAY

Using the song

★ Play track 20, demonstrating the actions (pg 45) and encouraging the children to join in and copy you.

★ Teach the whole song, asking the children to improvise their own actions as they sing.

★ Encourage the children to dance and 'boogie' in the instrumental verse at the end!

★ Show children the th card (pg 77) and say the sound together as in the words this and that. Can children identify words in the chorus containing th? (this, that, there, the.)

Child-initiated play

★ Ask the children to bring in photos of themselves as a baby, toddler and school child.

★ Share and discuss to extend vocabulary linked with moving and growing.

★ Provide the materials for them to create a portrait of themselves as cool teenagers.

Extend the activities

★ Show the children the lyrics of the whole song and ask them to identify any words they recognise.

★ Point out other high frequency words used in the verses and the choruses, eg a, was, little, this, when, I.

★ Make new verses for the song by substituting the lyrics and actions in the fourth line, eg 'When I was a tiny baby...I learned how to clap.'

What you will need

• Photographs
• Drawing materials
• Flashcard with digraph th (pg 77)

TEACHING FOCUS

★ Practising high frequency words
★ Consolidating the phoneme *th*
★ Generating new lyrics

SINGING PHONICS 2 © HELEN MACGREGOR & CATHERINE BIRT 2009 A&C BLACK PUBLISHERS LTD

THIS WAY, THAT WAY

When I was a tiny baby,
A baby, a baby,
When I was a tiny baby,
I learned how to crawl.
And I went...

This way,

Chorus:
This way, that way,
Up there, down there,
This way, that way,
The other way too.

That way,

When I was a little toddler,
A toddler, a toddler,
When I was a little toddler,
I learned how to walk,
And I went...
Chorus

Up there,

When I was a little school child,
A school child, a school child,
When I was a little school child,
I learned how to run.
And I went...
Chorus

Down there,

the other way, too

When I am a cool
teenager,
Teenager, teenager,
When I am a cool
teenager,
I'll learn how to dance.
And I'll go...
Chorus

Instrumental

HAVE YOU EVER?

Using the song

★ Play track 21 and encourage the children to join in straight away with the repeating lines (eg 'Have you ever seen a bat in a hat?'). Improvise simple actions as you all sing along.

★ Show the children the songsheet (pg 47) and ask them to identify familiar CVC words, eg bat, hat, vet, wet, jet, yak, mac, quack.

★ Teach the children the new digraphs – ee, oa, oo, ear - showing them each letter card. Sound talk the words from the song containing these new digraphs, eg s – ee- n, seen; g – oa - t, goat.

Child-initiated play

★ Encourage the children to sing the song, improvise actions and make up new rhyming verses.

★ Leave writing materials where the children can practise mark-making, using rhyming words.

Extend the activities

★ Explore the difference between the graphemes ee and ea, making the phoneme ee in the words bee, tree and see.

★ Create new verses with the children using a wider variety of phonemes, eg

> 'Bear without hair, sitting on the stair.'

> 'Snail on a whale, sitting on his tail'.

What you will need

• Letter cards with ee, oo, ear, oa (below, pg 48, 60 & 77)

ee

TEACHING FOCUS

★ Re-visiting simple cvc words and phonemes
★ Teaching new digraphs – *ee, oa, oo, ear* - and segmenting to spell and read
★ Generating new lyrics using a variety of phonemes/graphemes
★ Identifying rhyming words

SINGING PHONICS 2 © HELEN MACGREGOR & CATHERINE BIRT 2009 A&C BLACK PUBLISHERS LTD

HAVE YOU EVER?

Tune: If you're happy and you know it

Have you ever seen a bat in a hat?
Have you ever seen a bat in a hat?
Have you ever seen a bat, riding on a rat?
Have you ever seen a bat in a hat?

Have you ever seen a vet who was wet?
Have you ever seen a vet who was wet?
Have you ever seen a vet, flying in a jet?
Have you ever seen a vet who was wet?

Have you ever seen a yak in a mac?
Have you ever seen a yak in a mac?
Have you ever seen a yak, saying quack quack quack?
Have you ever seen a yak in a mac?

Have you ever seen a goat in a coat?
Have you ever seen a goat in a coat?
Have you ever seen a goat, building a big boat?
Have you ever seen a goat in a coat?

Have you ever seen a bee in the sea?
Have you ever seen a bee in the sea?
Have you ever seen a bee, talking to a tree?
Have you ever seen a bee in the sea?

Have you ever seen a fly wave goodbye?
Have you ever seen a fly wave goodbye?
Have you ever seen a fly, with a tear in his eye?
Have you ever seen a fly wave goodbye?

THE OO SONG

Using the song

★ Show the children the card and teach them the digraph oo.

★ Listen to the first verse of the song on track 22 or sing it yourself.

★ Ask the children to identify the words containing oo, eg soon, spoon, moon, moo, boo, balloon. Teach the first verse to the children.

★ Repeat the process with verse two (in the south of UK the children will notice a slight difference in pronunciation – a shorter vowel sound for the oo words).

Child-initiated play

★ Place the oo digraph card (below) and the picture cards (pg 49 or your own) where the children can play with them as they sing the song.

★ Provide picture books which contain illustrations of some of these words, eg Red Riding Hood, Hey diddle diddle, the Blue balloon, I want to see the moon.

★ Encourage the children to write captions or labels for the picture cards, eg moon and spoon.

Extend the activities

★ Play Postboxes: provide two simple postboxes made from cardboard boxes and a bag of artefacts, pictures and words containing the oo phoneme.

★ Ensure there is a mixture of the two pronunciations (long and short), eg wood, balloon, good, hook, food. Stick a picture on each postbox, eg boot and book.

★ To play the game, the children select an object, picture or word card from the bag and segment and blend the word before posting it into the appropriate box.

★ If possible, record the sounds you hear to take back and listen to later, or alternatively, take a photo or draw a picture of the sound source.

★ Play phoneme count together. Say whole words containing oo to the children, eg moon. Ask them to count the number of phonemes in the word by segmenting the sounds out loud to themselves. When you give them the signal they use their fingers or numbers cards to show you the answer,

eg m-oo-n (3), s-p-oo-n (4), b-a –ll-oo-n (5).

What you will need

- Card with digraph oo (below)
- Artefacts, picture cards and word cards of words containing oo, eg spoon, moon, balloon, hook, book
- Picture word cards (see pg 49) moon, balloon, hook, book
- Create your own flashcards using the blank cards on pg 71

TEACHING FOCUS

★ Teaching the new digraph oo
★ Teaching the two different pronunciations of the oo phonemes, eg spoon and hood
★ Practising and applying the new phonic skills and knowledge

THE OO SONG

Oo is in the middle of soon and spoon,
Oo is in the middle of moon.
Oo is at the end of moo and boo,
And it's somewhere inside a balloon.

Oo is in the middle of hook and look,
Oo is in the middle of took.
Oo is in the middle of hood and wood,
And it's somewhere inside a good book.

SUNSET

Using the song

★ Ask the children to read each of the six word cards by segmenting and blending.

★ Challenge them to see if they can make any longer words by combining two words from those given above (eg sunset or bedroom).

★ Collect their ideas. Listen to the song on track 23.

★ Do any of the words the children found appear in the song – sunset, tick tock or bedroom, or did they have other ideas as well, eg bedset, sunroom, tock-bed?

★ Teach the children the song one verse at a time, using the cards to remind them of the words.

Child-initiated play

★ Provide these six word cards so that the children can explore combining two to make longer words – real or made-up – to share with each other.

★ Add writing materials so that the children can practise writing the words on the cards.

Extend the activities

★ Show the children how they can combine other known CVC words to form longer words, eg ping-pong, carpark, cobweb, laptop, farmyard, boatman, rooftop.

★ Practise reading and writing them.

TEACHING FOCUS

★ Using two known CVC words to create two-syllable words
★ Reading two-syllable words

SUNSET

At the end of the day,
No more time to play,
'Cause it's sunset,   (sunset).

S – u – n   sun,
S – e – t   set,
Sunset,   (sunset).

S – u – n   sun,
S – e – t   set,
Sunset,   (sunset).

So it's off to bed,
Then I rest my head,
Hear the tick tock,   (tick tock).

T – i – ck   tick,
T – o – ck   tock,
Tick tock,   (tick tock).

T – i – ck   tick,
T – o – ck   tock,
Tick tock,   (tick tock).

Now I'm counting sheep,
Nearly fast asleep,
In my bedroom,   (bedroom).

B – e – d   bed,
R – oo – m   room,
Bedroom,   (bedroom).

B – e – d   bed,
R – oo – m   room,
Bedroom,   (bedroom).

sun

set

CITYSCAPE

Using the song

★ Listen to track 24 and ask the children to join in with the repeating phrases and sounds of the verses (eg 'Here comes a police car nee-naw nee-naw'.

★ Encourage the children to improvise. Teach the chorus line by line then perform the whole song.

★ Play the song again, encouraging the children to join in with the chosen vocal sounds in the appropriate places.

Child-initiated play

★ Provide props, building blocks, dressing up clothes, eg police hats, train driver's cap, to encourage the children to make sounds of the city during role play.

★ Set up a city area indoors or outdoors, or both to stimulate play and language development.

Extend the activities

★ Create new verses with the children, eg

'Here comes a red bus, ding ding, ding ding';

'Here comes a dustvan, sweep, sweep, sweep, sweep'.

★ Investigate some of the words through segmenting and blending, eg h-igh, high; h-igh-er, higher. Identify any new phonemes, eg ar & aw.

What you will need

- Toys - police car, tube train, bricks to make a tower-block
- Sound cards – nee-naw, zoom, high, higher (pgs 53 & 80)
- You can use blank flashcards (pg 71) and put in the new phonemes for the activity extension

TEACHING FOCUS

★ Practising and applying phonics skills and knowledge to read familiar and new words
★ Generating new verses to extend vocabulary

CITYSCAPE
Tune: Short'nin' bread

Chorus:
Busy city people all around,
See the sights and listen to the sound.
Busy city people all around,
See the sights and listen to the sound.

Here comes a police car nee-naw nee-naw,
Here comes a police car down the street.
Here comes a police car nee-naw nee-naw,
Here comes a police car down the street.

Chorus

Here comes a tube train, zoom zoom, zoom zoom,
Here comes a tube train, underground.
Here comes a tube train, zoom zoom, zoom zoom,
Here comes a tube train, underground.

Chorus

Up in the tower-block high, high, higher,
Up in the tower-block to the top.
Up in the tower-block high, high, higher,
Up in the tower-block to the top.

Chorus

PIRATES!

Using the song

★ Show the children the oi card (pg 78) as you teach the oi phoneme through the phrase 'Oi oi oi, it's ship ahoy!'

★ Listen to the song on track 25, asking the children to join in with this phrase which starts each repeat of the chorus: 'We're pirates bold and we're after gold'. Teach the rest of the chorus and sing it with track 25.

★ Teach the verses one at a time, at a later session if needed. Point out all the words which use the oi phoneme.

Child-initiated play

★ Provide a pirate's role-play area, outside if possible, with pirate words displayed as captions – coin, oi oi oi, hoist the sails, swab the decks, pieces of eight, pretty Polly, pirates bold, walk the plank, ship ahoy.

★ Encourage the children to make their own props, costumes, and write their own labels.

Extend the activities

★ Play Pirate's trash or treasure. Place a selection of golden coins as illustrated into the box displaying real and nonsense words such as coin, foil, soil, boib, noil.

★ Pass the box around as you sing the song. At the end of a verse or chorus, the child holding the box (the lucky pirate) chooses a word coin to segment and blend.

★ When the word has been deciphered the children decide whether it is trash or treasure and it is placed in the treasure box or trash can.

What you will need

• A treasure box and a trash can

• Card with oi (pg 78)

• Golden coins with oi phoneme words coin, join, coil, oil, toil, boil, soil, tinfoil, poison, boit, noit, zoit (photocopy and use the blank coin below)

TEACHING FOCUS

★ Teaching the new phoneme oi
★ Teaching oral segmenting and blending of new words containing the oi digraph
★ Discriminating between real and nonsense words containing oi

PIRATES!

Chorus:
Oi oi oi, it's ship ahoy,
Oi oi oi, me boys!
We're pirates bold and we're after gold,
As we sail the seven seas!

Yo ho ho, hoist the sails,
Yo ho ho, me boys!
We're pirates bold and we're after gold,
As we sail the seven seas!

Chorus

Swish swash swash, swab the decks,
Swish swash swash, me boys!
We're pirates bold and we're after gold,
As we sail the seven seas!

Chorus

Clink clunk clunk, count the coins,
Clink clunk clunk, me boys!
We're pirates bold and we're after gold,
As we sail the seven seas!

Chorus

THE STRANGE MACHINE

26

Using the song

★ Play track 26 or sing the song yourself, encouraging the children to join in straight away with the repeated sounds, adding spontaneous actions or movements if they wish.

Child-initiated play

★ Encourage children to work together in groups, acting out different parts of a machine, moving in rhythm to illustrate the actions suggested in the different verses.

★ The children may like to make up words for a new final verse in which the machine gets faster and faster and then blows up!

Extend the activities

★ Listen to the suggested sounds in each verse and think about what instruments or music makers would best represent these sounds, eg

Shakers for shake, shake, shake,

Large sheet of card for wobble, wobble, wobble.

★ Make up more verses using patterns of sound, eg

The strange machine went crash, bang, crash;

or

The strange machine went shake, rattle, roll.

★ Work with the children to create new imaginary machines which they can act out in movement and write new verses for the song:

'My pancake machine goes flip, flip, flop...'

'My washing machine goes swish, swish, swash...'

'My space machine goes woosh, woosh, woosh...'

'My games machine goes blip, blip, bleep...'

What you will need

• Instruments or music makers for the 'Extend the activities' section

TEACHING FOCUS

★ Experiencing and enjoying new vocabulary using a variety of phonemes
★ Experiencing rhythmic patterns of sound
★ Introducing the phoneme *er*

THE STRANGE MACHINE
Tune: There was a Princess long ago

The strange machine went click click click,
Click click click, click click click.
The strange machine went click click click,
Click click click.

The strange machine went toot toot toot,
Toot toot toot, toot toot toot.
The strange machine went toot toot toot,
Toot toot toot.

The strange machine went scrape scrape scrape,
Scrape scrape scrape, scrape scrape scrape.
The strange machine went scrape scrape scrape,
Scrape scrape scrape.

The strange machine went wobble wobble wobble,
Wobble wobble wobble, wobble wobble wobble.
The strange machine went wobble wobble wobble,
Wobble wobble wobble.

The strange machine went slower and slower,
Slower and slower, slower and slower.
The strange machine went slower and slower,
Slower, slower, stop!

RED RIDING HOOD RAP

Using the song

★ Ask the children to re-tell the story of Red Riding Hood using puppets if you wish. Listen to the chant on track 27 which tells the story.

★ Ask the children what they remember from the chant, playing it again if needed.

★ Invite the children to join in with the last line of each verse, using their voices expressively.

Child-initiated play

★ Provide simple props or puppets to encourage the children to re-enact the story.

★ Provide alternative versions of the story, including picture books, talking books, posters and big books for the children to explore and enjoy.

Extend the activities

★ Show the children the songsheet and ask them to identify familiar words or to attempt to segment and blend words to read.The children could use story maps to re-tell or act out the story in their own words.

★ Create a visual story map showing the main events in sequence. Annotate it with speech bubbles and other vocabulary suggested by the children.

What you will need

• Puppets (not essential)

• Picture books and stories, posters and big books for the 'Child-initiated play' section.

TEACHING FOCUS

★ Practising applying phonic skills and knowledge to re-tell a traditional tale
★ Experiencing a wide range of vocabulary
★ Experiencing and enjoying rhythm and rhyme

SINGING PHONICS 2 © HELEN MACGREGOR & CATHERINE BIRT 2009 **A&C BLACK PUBLISHERS LTD**

RED RIDING HOOD RAP

Now once upon a time,
In a cottage in a wood,
Lived a cute little girl,
Red Riding Hood.
CUTE GIRL!

Now one fine day,
Her Mum said to her,
Just take those goodies,
To your Grandmother.
KIND GIRL!

So off she set,
Through the deep dark wood,
The brave little girl,
Red Riding Hood.
BRAVE GIRL!

'Isn't that heavy?'
The ugly wolf asked her,
I'll take them,
'Cause I'll get there faster!'
CRAFTY WOLF.

He knocked Granny's door,
She shot out of bed,
'Get in the cupboard'
That bad wolf said.
WICKED WOLF!

Along came Little Red Riding Hood,
To see her Grandmother if she could,
'What big ears, big teeth, big eyes'
Altogether a scary surprise.
UGLY WOLF!

The woodcutter heard,
Red Riding Hood shout,
So he gave the wolf,
A jolly big clout.
BRAVE WOODCUTTER!

The wolf was shocked,
And he took fright,
Out popped Grandma,
What a sight.
POOR GRANDMA!

No more wolf,
To scare them away,
Just a nice big party,
With time to play.
HOORAY!
HOORAY!

HAPPY ENDINGS

Using the song

★ Show the children the ow card as you teach them the first verse. Can they remember the three words which end with ow used in the song? (cow, how, now.)

★ Can they think of others which rhyme, eg row, sow, bow, pow.

★ Repeat this process with the other verses until the children are familiar with the whole song.

Child-initiated play

★ Leave the ow, ear, air, ure ending words cards used in the song along with writing equipment so that the children can practise reading and writing known and new vocabulary.

Extend the activities

★ Play a game. Find the words that end with ow as an oral activity or using picture cards/objects.

★ Create new verses for later stages of phonic development, eg words which end with:

      oy – boy, toy and joy;

      ay - say, hay and play;

      ng - string, thing and sing.

What you will need

• Four cards with the digraph ow and trigraphs ear, air and ure. (below and pg 78)

TEACHING FOCUS

★ Introducing the new digraph – ow
★ Introducing the new trigraphs (three letters making one phoneme) – ear, air, ure
★ Application of new phonic skills in reading and writing

60   *SINGING PHONICS 2 © HELEN MACGREGOR & CATHERINE BIRT 2009* **A&C BLACK PUBLISHERS LTD**

HAPPY ENDINGS
Tune: Skip to my Lou

We love words that end with ow,
We love words that end with ow,
We love words that end with ow,
Like cow and how and wow!
Ow, ow, ow, ow, ow,
Ow, ow, ow, ow, ow,
Ow, ow, ow, ow, ow,
Cow and how and wow!

We love words that end with ear, (x3)
Like dear and hear and near.
Ear, ear, ear, ear, ear, (x3)
Dear and hear and near.

We love words that end with air, (x3)
Like chair and hair and air.
Air, air, air, air, air, (x3)
Chair and hair and air.

We love words that end with ure. (x3)
Like cure and pure and sure,
Ure, ure, ure, ure, ure, (x3)
Cure and pure and sure.

ow ear air ure

MELODY LINES

CAN YOU SIT UPON A PIN?

TAP TAP TAP

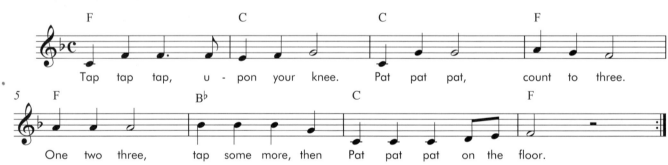

PASS THE HAT - Row row row your boat

SINGING PHONICS 2 © HELEN MACGREGOR & CATHERINE BIRT 2009 A&C BLACK PUBLISHERS LTD

YOO HOO HOO - The Hokey Cokey

With a swing

You say the *b* sound first, And then the *a* sound too. You
fin - ish with the *t* sound and give a yoo hoo hoo! You put the sounds to - ge - ther then you
wait and see,___ What will the new word be? Oh, we can make a
new word,___ Oh, we can make a new word,___
Oh, we can make a new word,___ *b - a - t* makes bat, you see!

TICK TOCK

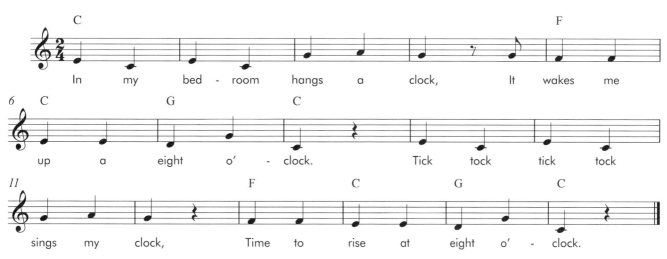

In my bed - room hangs a clock, It wakes me
up a eight o' - clock. Tick tock tick tock
sings my clock, Time to rise at eight o' - clock.

RUN RAT RUN

ROCKET DOG - The bear went over the mountain

SAD MAD CATS

Sad mad cats, In black silk hats, Are mar-ching in-to town.

Meow meow, meow meow, Mar-ching up and down.

BIG BAD BUG

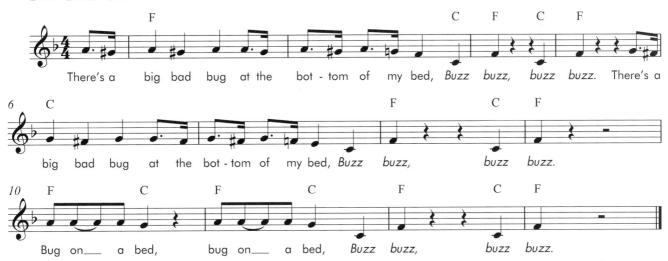

There's a big bad bug at the bot-tom of my bed, Buzz buzz, buzz buzz. There's a

big bad bug at the bot-tom of my bed, Buzz buzz, buzz buzz.

Bug on__ a bed, bug on__ a bed, Buzz buzz, buzz buzz.

DOUBLES

With a swing

Dou-bles at the end Dou-bles at the end, Dou-ble ff,

that says f, In huff and puff and stuff.

SECRET ANIMAL - Wind the bobbin up

Se - cret a - ni - mal, se - cret a - ni - mal, Hop hop hop hop
hop. See all the a - ni - mals one two three, Wolf, snake, rab - bit
which will it be? (spoken) It's the rabbit! Se - cret
a - ni - mal, se - cret a - ni - mal, Hop hop hop hop hop.

ALPHABET

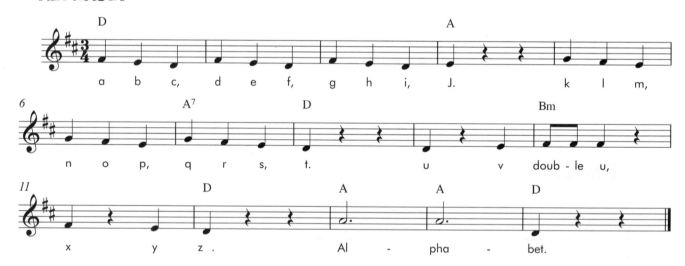

a b c, d e f, g h i, J. k l m,
n o p, q r s, t. u v doub - le u,
x y z . Al - pha - bet.

TWENTY SIX LETTERS - Ten green bottles

Twen-ty six lett-ers___ in the al-pha-bet, Twen-ty six lett-ers___ in the al-pha-bet, For-ty four pho nemes, This is what we get! Twen ty six lett ers__ in the al-pha-bet. Can you say the pho-nemes? c a t (Spoken) Can you say the pho-nemes? c a t (Spoken) Blend the sounds to geth-er,___ And let's see what we get. c a t (Spoken) make the new word cat.

HAM AND JAM

I like Pam and I like Sam, Pam and Sam like me. Pam and Sam or Sam and Pam, They're my pals, you see! Pam Sam Sam Pam, Pam and Sam like me. Pam Sam Sam Pam, They're my pals, you see!

MELODY LINES

DIZZY THE DINOSAUR

Di - zzy___ the di - no - saur dan - cing___ all day, Di - zzy___ the di - no - saur dan - cing___ this way, Jer - ky___ Ji - ving, Wob - bly___ wad - dling, Bu - sy bop - ping,___ not e - ven stop - ping.___ Di - zzy___ the di - no - saur dan - cing___ all day, Di - zzy___ the di - no - saur dan - cing___ this way.

CHEEKY CHIMP

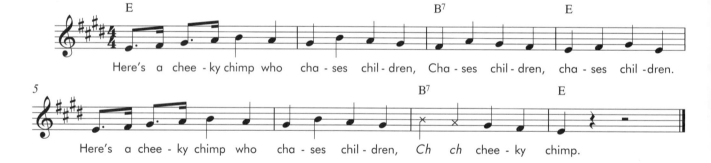

Here's a chee - ky chimp who cha - ses chil - dren, Cha - ses chil - dren, cha - ses chil - dren. Here's a chee - ky chimp who cha - ses chil - dren, *Ch ch* chee - ky chimp.

SH!

My mys - tery box has some - thing to hide, The pho - neme is *sh* Some where in - side, With fins and a tail, it swims in the sea, What do you think this *sh* word can be? It's a *f - i - sh* fish
(Spoken)

 SINGING PHONICS 2 © HELEN MACGREGOR & CATHERINE BIRT 2009 **A&C BLACK PUBLISHERS LTD**

KING PING PONG

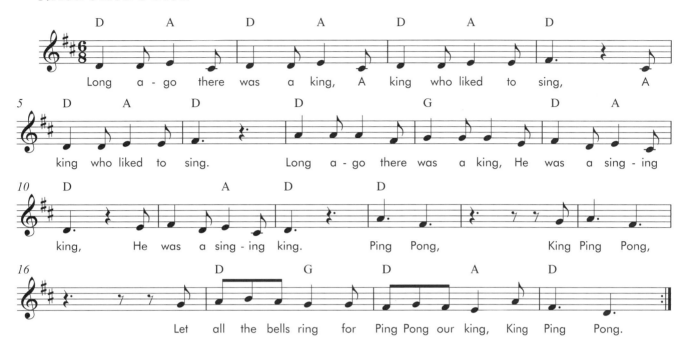

THIS WAY THAT WAY

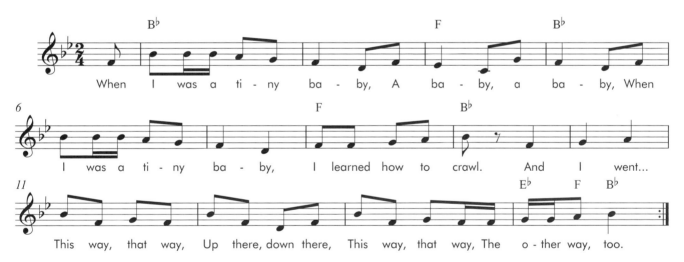

HAVE YOU EVER? – If you're happy and you know it

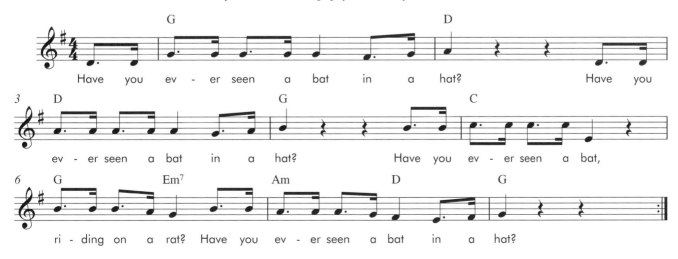

THE OO SONG

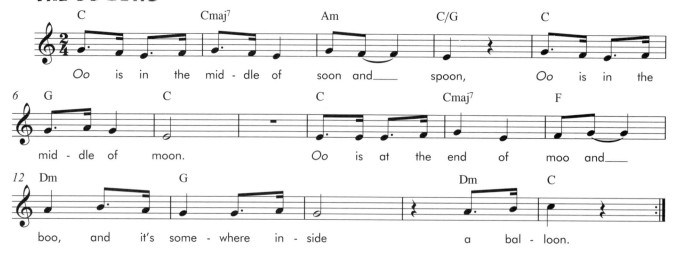

Oo is in the mid-dle of soon and spoon, Oo is in the mid-dle of moon. Oo is at the end of moo and boo, and it's some-where in-side a bal-loon.

SUNSET

At the end of the day, No more time to play, 'Cause it's sun-set, (sun-set). s-u-n sun, s-e-t set, Sun-set. (sun-set).

CITYSCAPE – Short'nin' bread

Bu-sy ci-ty peo-ple all a-round, See the sights and lis-ten to the sound. Bu-sy ci-ty peo-ple all a-round, See the sights and lis-ten to the sound. Here comes a po-lice car nee-naw nee-naw, Here comes a po-lice car down the street. Here comes a po-lice car nee-naw nee-naw, Here comes a po-lice car down the street

PIRATES!

Oi oi oi, it's ship a - hoy, Oi oi oi, me boys! We're pi - rates bold and we're af - ter gold, As we sail the se - ven____ seas! Yo ho ho, hoist the sails, Yo ho ho, me boys! We're pi - rates bold and we're af - ter gold, As we sail the se - ven____ seas!

THE STRANGE MACHINE - There was a Princess long ago

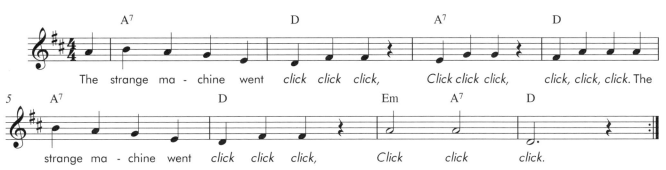

The strange ma - chine went click click click, Click click click, click, click, click. The strange ma - chine went click click click, Click click click.

HAPPY ENDINGS - Skip to my Lou

We love words that end with - ow, We love words that end with - ow, We love words that end with - ow, Like cow and how and wow! Ow, ow, ow, ow, ow, Ow, ow, ow, ow, ow, Ow, ow, ow, ow, ow, Cow and how and wow!

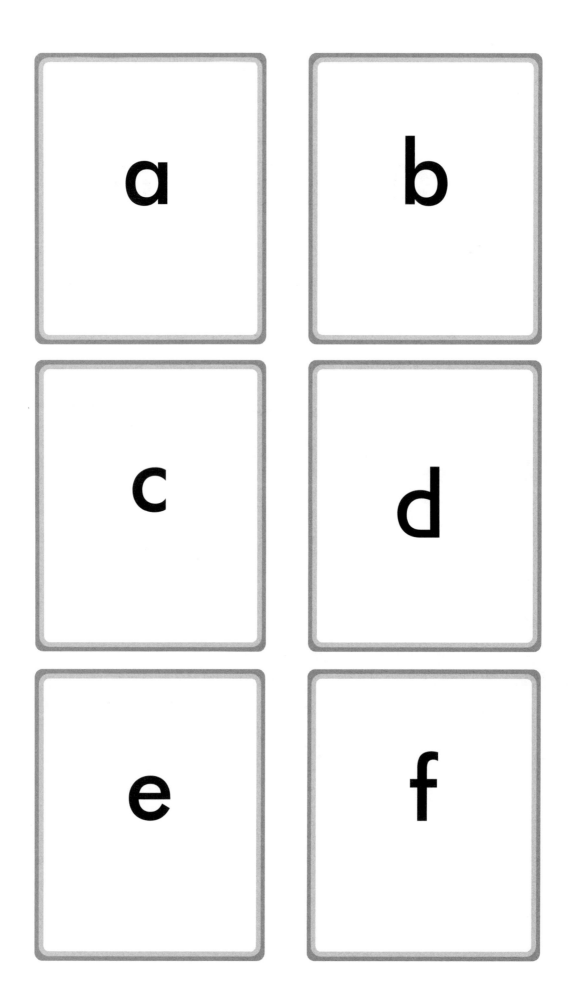

a

b

c

d

e

f

 SINGING PHONICS 2 © HELEN MACGREGOR & CATHERINE BIRT 2009 **A&C BLACK PUBLISHERS LTD**

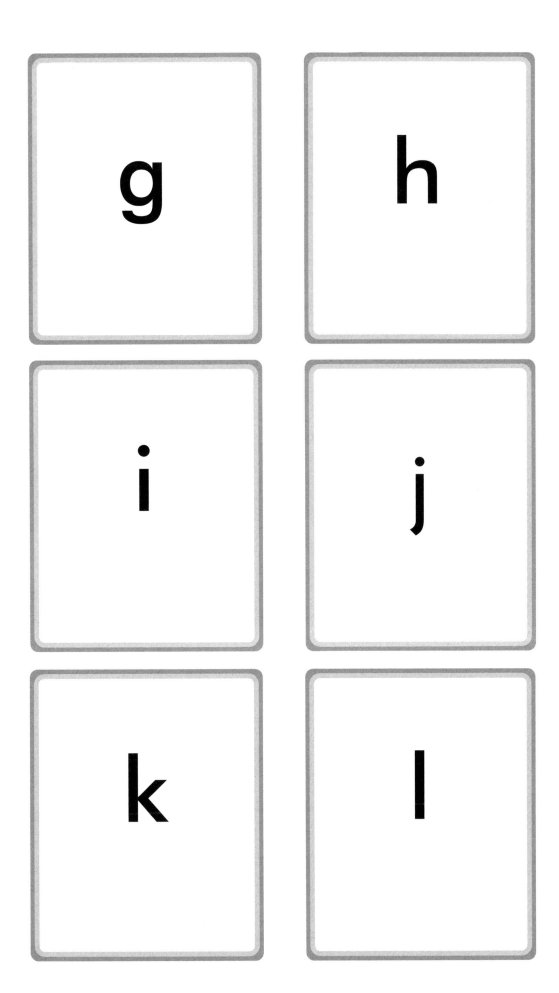

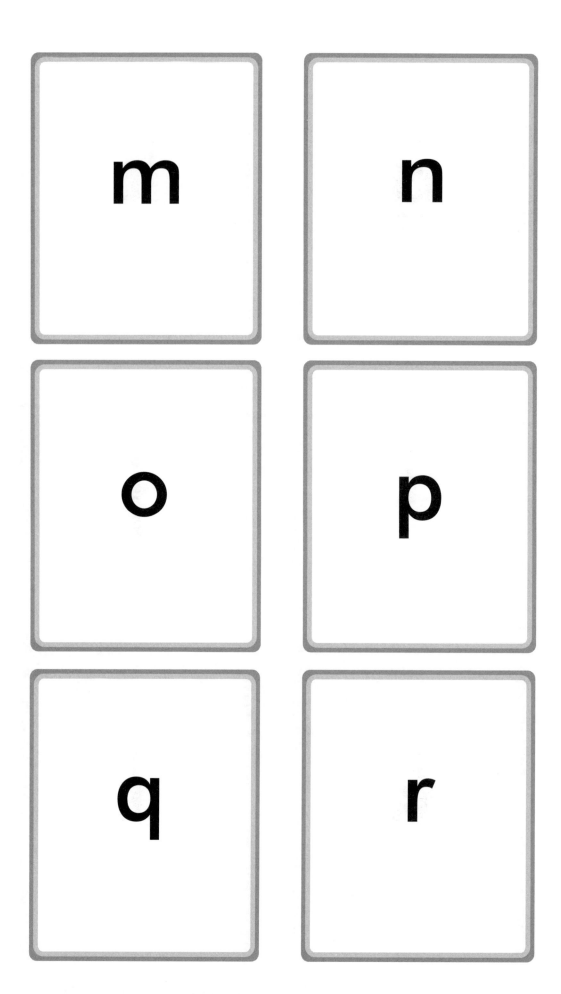

m

n

o

p

q

r

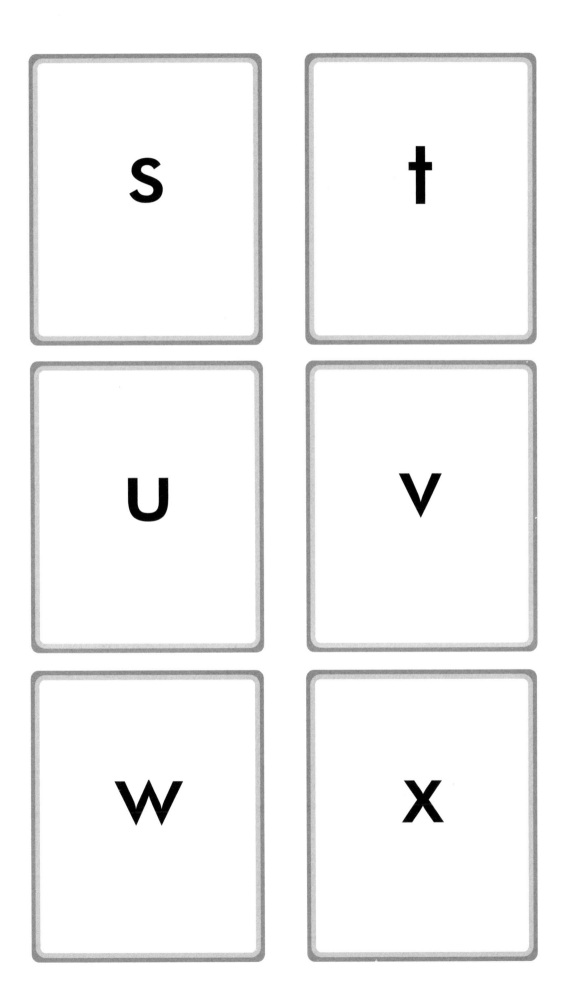

s

t

u

v

w

x

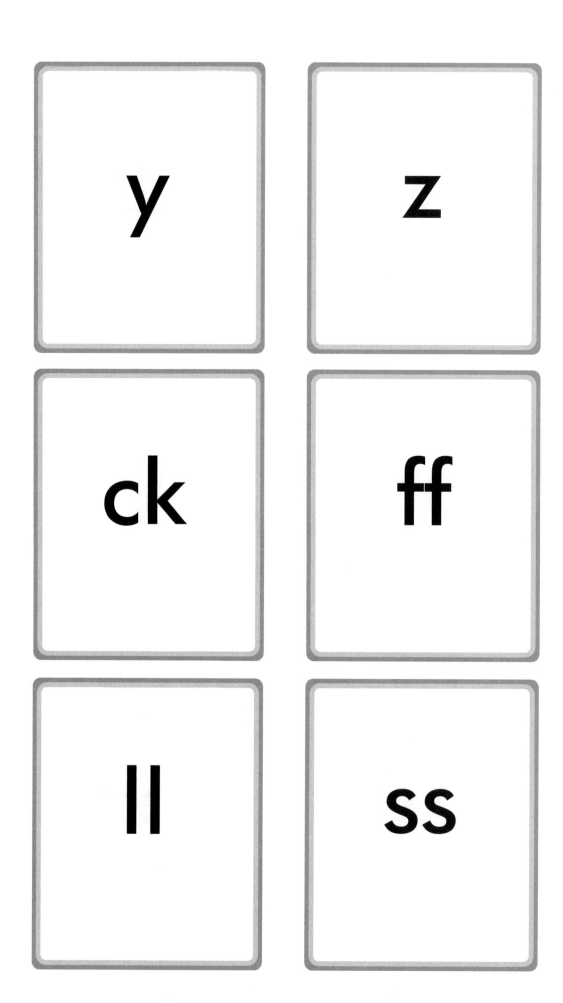

y

z

ck

ff

ll

ss

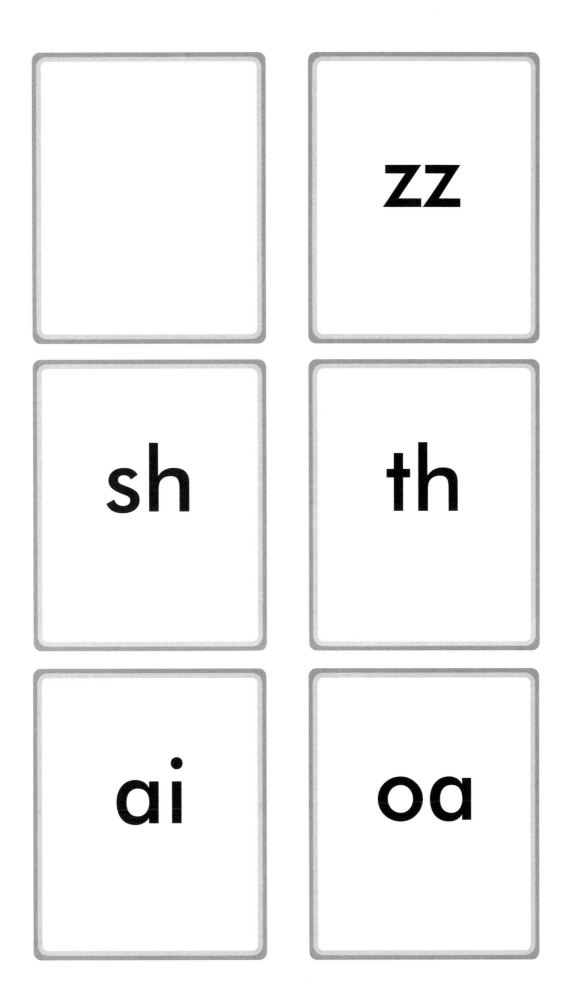

zz

sh

th

ai

oa

or

air

oi

ure

er

well

kiss

miss

shell

bell

fuzz

fizz

Sam

fun

bed

room

zoom